Bugs, Bugs, Bugs!

Walkingsticks

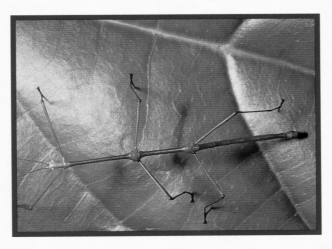

by Fran Howard

Consulting Editor: Gail Saunders-Smith, PhD

Consultant: Gary A. Dunn, MS, Director of Education
Young Entomologists' Society Inc.
Lansing, Michigan

Capstone press

Mankato, Minnesota

Pebble Plus is published by Capstone Press,
1710 Roe Crest Drive, P.O. Box 669, North Mankato, Minnesota 56003.
www.capstonepub.com

 Books published by Capstone Press are manufactured with paper
containing at least 10 percent post-consumer waste.

Library of Congress Cataloging-in-Publication Data
Howard, Fran, 1953–
    Walkingsticks/by Fran Howard.
    p. cm.—(Pebble plus: bugs, bugs, bugs!)
    Includes bibliographical references and index.
    ISBN-13: 978-0-7368-3645-6 (hardcover)   ISBN-10: 0-7368-3645-4 (hardcover)
    ISBN-13: 978-0-7368-5103-9 (softcover)   ISBN-10: 0-7368-5103-8 (softcover)
    1. Stick insects—Juvenile literature. I. Title. II. Series.
QL509.5.H68 2005
595.7′29—dc22   2004011972

Summary: Simple text and photographs describe the physical characteristics of walkingsticks.

Editorial Credits

Sarah L. Schuette, editor; Linda Clavel, set designer; Kate Opseth, book designer; Kelly Garvin,
    photo researcher; Scott Thoms, photo editor

Photo Credits

Bruce Coleman Inc./David T. Overcash, 5; Donald Mammoser, 6–7; E. R. Degginger, 9; Michael Fogden, 10–11
Corel, 1
David Liebman/Dennis Sheridan, 17
Dwight R. Kuhn, 21
Image Ideas Inc., back cover (leaf)
ImageWest/Jeffrey M. Greene, 15
James P. Rowan, 13
McDonald Wildlife Photography/Joe McDonald, cover
Nature Picture Library/Pete Oxford, 18–19
Photodisc, back cover (walkingstick)

Note to Parents and Teachers

The Bugs, Bugs, Bugs! set supports national science standards related to the diversity of
life and heredity. This book describes and illustrates walkingsticks. The images support
early readers in understanding the text. The repetition of words and phrases helps early
readers learn new words. This book also introduces early readers to subject-specific
vocabulary words, which are defined in the Glossary section. Early readers may need
assistance to read some words and to use the Table of Contents, Glossary, Read More,
Internet Sites, and Index sections of the book.

Printed in the United States of America in North Mankato, Minnesota.
052012   006719R

Table of Contents

What Are Walkingsticks?

Walkingsticks are long,

thin insects.

How Walkingsticks Look

Walkingsticks look like
sticks that can walk.
Most walkingsticks are gray,
brown, or green.

Walkingsticks are about
as long as a child's hand.

Walkingsticks have six legs.

They walk very slowly.

Walkingsticks have

two antennas.

Walkingsticks use antennas

to feel and smell.

What Walkingsticks Do

Walkingsticks eat plants
and leaves.

Walkingsticks lay eggs

on plants.

Young walkingsticks hatch

after a few years.

Walkingsticks sway

in the wind

to hide from birds.

Birds eat walkingsticks.

Some walkingsticks hide
on plants.
They change color
to look like the plant.